T0147346

The Waiting Room Chronicles

The Waiting Room Chronicles

Individual death illustrated as an absurdist continuous cycle

By

PERRY L. ANGLE

iUniverse, Inc.
Bloomington

THE WAITING ROOM CHRONICLES
Individual death illustrated as an absurdist continuous cycle

iUniverse books may be ordered through booksellers or by contacting:

iUniverse
1663 Liberty Drive
Bloomington, IN 47403
www.iuniverse.com
1-800-Authors (1-800-288-4677)

ISBN: 978-1-4620-5424-4 (sc)
ISBN: 978-1-4620-5425-1 (ebk)

Library of Congress Control Number: 2011916340

Printed in the United States of America

iUniverse rev. date: 09/27/2011

Dedication

To
Ashley, Alex, Anslee, Zoie and Claire
My Grand Assortment
Long and happy life to all my darlings

Think of all the supposed or little understood bodies we can only conjecture to exist—black dwarfs, dark energy, the Chameleon Force Hawking radiation, gravitons, gluons, Higgs particles, Strings, new planet formations in extra solar space such as HD 37605b in Orion as well as

HEAVEN

FOREWORD

Philosophers since the time of the writer Origen and others have visited the idea of the Pool of Souls. It has fostered much conjecture. Simply stated after death the soul is recycled. In science, this is similar to the idea of the Conservation of Matter which states that "Matter is neither created nor destroyed but simply changed in form". An example might be an ice cube which can be solid, or vapor (gas-like), or water.

The Waiting Room Chronicles explores this idea and incorporates some diverse religious doctrine in an effort to illustrate this unique concept. I have always been fascinated by the interplay of religion, mythology, science and philosophy. For instance there are a number of flood stories in mythology and in the literature of various cultures which can be found in religious teaching. The story describes an absurdist cyclicality based upon an unrealistic confidence in Hope.

This volume includes some poetry and prose which offers a satirical portrayal of our human condition. Also, a short story The Jubilee, further explores the interplay of mythology and religion. It takes place in Alabama during an unusual and isolated southern phenomenon called a jubilee. The poem 2012 revisits an idea of Plato's. Other poetry and prose illustrate the inescapable conclusion that progress may have helped to define our world at the expense of our values.

The author hopes and believes his reader will find the book to be entertaining, instructive and thought provoking and provide an insight into the nature and basis of belief systems. After all, that has been the aim of philosophy throughout the ages.

THE WAITING ROOM

A play in two acts

By

Perry L. Angle

June 2006

CAST OF CHARACTERS

The Messenger   Jesus

Sword   A soldier

Dominique   A Creole voodoo queen

Akmed   A professor and tutor

Sunshine   A follower of Buddha

Sandy   A smuggler and sometimes Taoist

Parson   A Negro, self-ordained preacher

ACT ONE

Scene 1

A large room without windows. It is early morning. The only light comes from outside the door. It is a low continuous beam which intensifies only in the presence of the messenger. Wooden stools against each wall are the only furniture. The room is wide and spacious.

In it, a number, in fact, quite a number of bored, tired people are waiting for their next assignment. There is a single door and the lower part does not touch the floor—a gap of a half-foot is left so that the messenger may pass the assignment and any special instructions in a plain brown 8 x 10 envelope marked with the alpha-numeric name of the individual to be chosen.

In the foreground, nearest the door, a man sits with his legs folded under him. His palms are turned outward. He is rotund and rocks to and fro as if in some orchestrated rhythmic response to an unseen stimulus. His hair is white and unkempt. He similes politely at the Negro woman across from him.

She is standing and staring at the wallpaper which is a totality of smiley faces, the same that children love to stick on anything they can find.

The yellow sea of smiley faces undermines the seriousness of the room. She is not amused and frowns. The long, flower sack dress has seen much wear. Her hair is jet black but tinged with gray and held in place by an African headband with a variation of voodoo symbols. The dress is torn down one side so that her thighs are visible.

Another is knelling on the floor in an attitude of prayer. His knees are shaking. The floor is cement and his face shows twinges of pain. He is a Negro—tall with a long, unkempt, gray beard. His face is scared by a welt.

One is dressed in a soldier's uniform and sleeps. There are many others but they do not concern us now. Except for one other who suddenly appears in their midst. He arrives just as a loud noise is heard. He is the first to speak.

Za-penng

"Well, I'm back. Can't say that I'm happy about it. Why are you people staring at me? You know the routine. Za-penng, you're here. Za-penng, your gone. That old invisible bungee cord snapping you here and there."

He snaps his fingers and says. I'll have a bit of sake and suddenly he has a glass of sake in his hand.

That is the only good thing about this damn waiting room. You can have anything you wish for except freedom, happiness or death.

He drops exhausted onto a wooden stool.

What is your name? Asks the Negro woman.

Alpha 152262m, he replies.
Where do you come from and what did you do?

Does it matter? I do what I am told. If you must know, I was a smuggler in the south China sea and other places. I smuggled people to Macau during the Japanese invasion of Shanghai. I loved danger. The Japanese were ruthless. It was a bad time.

Za-penng

Hey look, way down the room. Another fellow just came in. Got his head in his hands. Well there, now he's put it back on again. Too far down the hall to talk to but the way he is dressed, I'll bet he was an aristocrat in the old Reign of Terror.

Negro Woman	Yes, all of us are familiar with terror—our constant companion. How many times have you been down, Alpha 152262m?
Alpha 152262m	Hey, we gotta find a better way to communicate. That's their idea not mine. I prefer my first name. First time I remember I had a name.
Negro Woman	What was it?
Alpha 152262	Sandy, I think cause I use to land my cargo on unwatched sandy beaches. What's your name?
Negro Woman Beta 62402j	Just call me, Dominique. You must have just been caught.
Sandy	Yeah. I made a number of runs but last night I was intercepted on a beach landing. They killed my passengers and then hung me from the mainmast.
Dominique	Did you suffer much?
Sandy	Rope burned hard on my neck. They used a short rope so they could watch me dance.

Sandy lowers his shirt to expose his throat which is badly bruised and raw where the rope had cut the flesh.

B14o   Hey, done like Billy Budd, or Hale or Captain Kidd.

A second, a minute, an hour what difference—just swinging in the breeze
and Za-penng here you are. I say, lucky they didn't hang you from an old
Cottonwood tree. You could still be swinging. Saw that once when I was
a coolie in the mining camps in California. My name is B14o and I am
here to tell you it's all suffering and pain. Suffering that's the crux of it.
Our lot—each and all of us.

Dominique   Shut up you old fool.

Sandy, don't mind old B14o. We call him Sunshine.

Haven't got no idea why. I guess cause way he talks like he ain't never
known a moments hope.

Sunshine Hope, you say. Who needs it? Useless here! You can damn well
see that. Last item in Pandora's box, it was. By the time hope got out all
the ills were bed rocked. For me, pain is a boon—only constant a man
can know.
Learn to love it.

Dominique   Sandy, how many times?

Sandy   Oh, yeah, I forgot, three for sure. I remember one that's
             a bit vague but it reminds me of the sea and I think that
             I was happy there and then I think I may have been
             shipwrecked. As I said, all vague.

Guess as a Negro you had your share of times. I was an Oriental last time
but I chose my route to distress. At least, insofar as choice is allowed after
you have been assigned.

And I wore your color once. Nothing good came of it. Have a drink. We can talk.

Dominique says Jax and a can of beer pops in her hand. Salute, Sandy.

He makes an appropriate motion and drinks.

Theta 666sx   We are all sinners—waiting here in the waiting room. If I had my way, I'd wait for death. Wish for it. Can't have it, so I won't. Got to go back, unfinished business as always.

Sandy   Whose he?

Sandy pops his fingers again and his glass is filled.

Dominique   We call him parson. Don't know whether he is a preacher or not. Negro, like me. Could be ordained but I doubt it. Look at his hands—hands of a field hand. All I could get out of him was that he held prayer sessions in the ante-bellum south just as they went into the cotton fields.

She looks at him and says COTTON and instantly the floor around him is littered with picked cotton.

Happy, now parson?

Parson   Thank you kindly, sister. God made it white for purity. Best things I ever seen are white—cotton, clouds, snow and peoples at least happy peoples. If hope were a color, it would be white too.

Lord God, how I loved that ole King Cotton and all my peoples loved it too. Fill them croaker sacks and praise the lawd while we's picking. Picking the white King Cotton in the red clay fields of Georgia. Amen.

Dominique   Amen!

Sandy   Parson mentioned he wanted to die but he's done it already. I can clap my hands and have any tangible thing I want. But here I can't have happiness, freedom or death. All other things are possible. I said that before, didn't I? It's true!

Dominique looks at Sandy and feels a deep need for him. He, she thinks, could be the one she could love. He could be the gentle touch she longs for—despite a lust that consumes her.

Dominique   Maybe, in another time to come. We could be real friends. I'd like that.

Sunshine interrupts any response from Sandy.

Sunshine   You know why, those things are denied? Even love for you sister. I see lust in your eyes. Can't have what you want. Cause time is a convenience. Even with the best atomic clock with Cesium innards, you can't have your desires. Time is a name we give to a condition, an ever-flowing movement, an energy force. Forget your desires, subdue them. Everything depends on something. Nothing by itself exists even inanimate it is dependent upon something—the gravestone you sleep under is dependent upon the sod to support it. Einstein proved time can be slowed or accelerated because it is a condition we observe and none of us are in the same observable position. Remember the old Za-penng.

Dominique   Old buzzard, you are too pessimistic for me.

Sunshine   No, I am too realistic for you. Let it go. The reason you cannot die is because you are dependent upon something in this purgatorial intermission.

Sandy   Say you are right. What is it that controls us? What is the purpose of this?

Sunshine   For epistemological, teleological and ontological answers I refer you to the messenger's employer whoever he is and wherever he may reside. All I know is we are all going back because that is the way we are programmed. In a sense, like a damn chip.

Za-penng.

Sunshine   There goes another one. Think it was that guy who had to put his head back on. Ole headless! He went quick. I don't like bright light especially that light that floods the room when the messenger comes to the door. Guess, I wasn't watching when headless got his envelope.

Sunshine says tree and snaps his fingers and a tall tree rises next to him and gives him shade.

I'll bet headless was meant for the blue room and somehow got routed here and they pulled him back.

Another thing, I don't like smiley faces. Accentuates the damn joke.

Sandy	Dominique, what was your last trip like?
Dominique	Well, I had a rough time. I was a little girl and my mom took me on this pilgrimage to a seaport town in Haiti. It was a voodoo march. Much drinking and fornicating, hell-raising time it was. Worse, there were orgies in the graveyard. I was awed by it. I felt drawn to it. I was only 15 but that last night I was brutally and repeatedly raped. It was insanity, murder, rape, mayhem—hideous, painted, laughing faces in the dark.

Later, I had a child from that night. I named him Specter. He died young from some damn fever. May have been Cholera.

Sandy	What did you do then?
Dominique	I became a prostitute and eventually a voodoo queen. Man could I cast a spell. I spelled a man real bad, so bad it took him a long time to die. I enjoyed it because I knew him as one of the ones who took me that night on the slab. One night, I was spaced out on hallucinogens. His wife entered my room and slit my throat. What I regret most is that I never knew love. Never had a man in a fulfilling way. Never was I able to welcome the intruder.
Parson	Got time now sister. Bring peace and love into your life, let Jesus in.
Dominique	Shut up, you old fool. You don't know him any more than the rest of us do. He got snapped back on the old

bungee cord just like the rest of us. And he died violent just like the rest of us. That's all we got in commons with him.

Parson   I got hope. I'm gonna get dat prize. Next assignment, I'll be happy, have a long life, maybe a cotton farm and hit be all mine or a fine country church. He won't let me down this time cause I been praying to him. I already been down four times. Once in dat big war. Died in a charge agin those confederates but lawad done told me bear no hate fer em.

Sunshine   Only prize, you gonna get old darky is what you already got, a chance to taste death. Hell, even the most bitter fruit won't be as bitter after you taste it a few more times.

He snaps his finger and says pomegranate and tries to hand it to the parson.

Dominique   You old bastard, you watch how you treat him or I'll put the gris-gris on you.

Parson   No sir, Mr. Sunshine. Thanks be but I don't want hit.

Sandy   That was the fruit in the Garden of Eden. Not a damn apple. Also, the only tree in hell. Ask Persephone, about what happens to him who tastes it. Good for you, parson.

Dominique   Sandy, what do you know about that soldier? He's been sleeping quite a time."

Sandy	He came in yesterday. You came right after him and didn't notice. Said, he fought against the Canaanites at Megiddo with Tutmose III. That's all I know. Oh, he did say he was tired of fighting in ancient times. Wanted to fight in a more recent time. Expecting to be a soldier again. His fourth time. Did say, he fought one battle at Khartoum. Also, he had that vague recollection of a quiet sea and being shipwrecked.
Dominique	I had that same notion.
Sunshine	It was your sin cast you ashore, expelled you, expelled us all from that amniotic sea that for us is an archetype—a universal. Like Aphrodite we were born from froth and foam. The sea coughed us up at the appropriate time.

Suddenly, the soldier sits up. He glares at Sunshine with an unmistaken hate. And shakes his fist at him.

Tau 742p	Make no mistake. I will eviscerate you if you continue. I heard every word. You are the worst of us and we are all a sorry lot so take no satisfaction in it but make no more such outbursts or I shall carve you before the messenger comes. You will not dampen my enthusiasm. The prize will be mine.
Sandy	We do not like these names. We shall call you, Sword. May I say that you must feel as I do that something binds us together. That within this room we are part of a common denominator—what is it?
Sword	Can't say, but something, I agree.

Parson	We all died and more than once with hard deaths.
Sandy	Yes, and we are all aware of some vague event on or near a sea that is as loudmouth said for us an archetype. Most probably that amniotic sea, he mentioned. Yet, I don't know what it means. Sunshine, we know nothing of you, did you die a violent death as well?
Sword	He may yet have another.
Sunshine	Yes, violent. My first assignment took me to India. I was a member of that caste group known as the untouchables. All the dirty jobs were ours. We were considered unclean. It was our lot to clean sewers or other low jobs. We were shunned. I died horribly from a cancer that left me covered in lesions. Sepsis put an end to it finally.

Parson mumbles, my Job he had dem lesions. God give him hard task.

Sunshine	Yet, there was in it a sense I had of being a pawn in a historical play, that I would experience life out of my experience, that I would cross boundaries and in my next life I had become something else again. Can you not see what I mean? You asked what brings us together, us and all the myriads in this room. I will tell you. We have in each life crossed a barrier, in a sense experienced life out of our expected boundary. In some sense, we ooze through the history of man. You will suffer again and again, and again. Suffering is our lot.

Za-penng

13

Another joins them. He stands and wipes sleep from his eyes then focuses on Dominique. He is brown skinned and wears a gray pair of trousers, a white shirt-with many blood stains and red suspenders.

Dominique   Hello, welcome. Your name, please. Where are you from?

Zeta 661d   I am called Akmed and was by profession, a private tutor to a sheik and his three sons. I was trained in a university in Europe. I taught the usual academic slate but my mandate was to teach philosophy to his children.

Sandy   Why, didn't he have his own philosophy? One he had to pass on, some Arab doctrine?

Akmed   Of course that, but he wanted his children exposed to the thoughts of the world from Plato and Aristotle to the moderns. I am afraid that I did badly and he had me beheaded. I was known as Zeta 661d but prefer Akmed.

Sunshine   We saw another fellow earlier enter headless.

Akmed   I could remove mine if you wish.

Dominique and Sandy both scream no.

Sunshine   Why as you say, did you do badly. It is hard to mess up Philosophy?

Akmed   I taught them existentialism and with enough enthusiasm that one of his sons became a convert. So the sheik had me beheaded and his son exiled. I would do it again. I have found comfort in the freedom it offers. Even this absurdist cyclically does not interrupt my pleasure in its tenants. If there is a next assignment, I shall be as I am.

Sunshine	Sad philosophy to die for. One of your members said that "Man was condemned to be free". There is no freedom in the cyclicality of existence, in being perpetually re-assigned—yet, one can be free if he achieves that blessed state of enlightenment. Only that philosophy breaks the rope of bondage.
Akmed	Something you obviously have not done.
Parson	My sweet lawd, will set you free.

Parson stands and Dominique gasps. The old Negro has half his right foot missing.

Parson	Ah sister, easy. Overseer done it. Caught me on the railroad, brought me back and chopped it off so's I couldn't run no mo. Dat was in my last life. I started preaching after dat.
Akmed	Considering the modern cell phone dominated, credit card using, bargain sale hunting, MSG consuming society that has evolved, I prefer to hold myself in contempt of it all. I have no desire for another assignment. The world has outgrown its resources. The air and water are my enemies. Man contaminated his garden.
Sunshine	And by that, you are damned.

Akmed	Yes, admittedly so, as I am part of the company of men. A company I detest but to which I am bound. I bear the guilt both of existence and of essence as the chicken or the egg is culpable by default.
Sandy	How by existence?
Akmed	By a sin of another long ago in an orchard.
Sandy	How by essence?
Akmed	I made of myself this pitiful recluse now before you. Every path I took I did so consciously and with purpose insofar as choice was permitted. Now, forgive me. I need solitude.

Akmed turns his back on the others and begins to paint a mural over the smiley faces and says nothing more. Sunshine bites into the pomegranate and makes a face and Dominique runs to Sandy and hugs him as the curtain falls.

ACT TWO

For a few moments, no one speaks. Dominique continues to embrace Sandy and snaps her finger for a beer.

Further down the room, three elderly men are racing matchbox cars. The tree that shades sunshine is beginning to droop and some leaves have fallen. Sandy has another sake. More Za-penngs are heard outside their room. Sandy studies the mural.

It is a circle and inscribed within the circle is an Ankh and a DNA helix with an infinity symbol between them .And on both sides of the circle are tombstones. Ahmed finishes and looks about for approval.

Sandy Hey, Akmed, nice mural, small but interesting. Life from the ancients and from the modern symbolically stated both with the same message. Nice!

Akmed Thanks, Sunshine said we ooze through history, in a sense we evolve through it—the infinity symbol in the center placed there because we can't define the inexplicable without experience which is impossible to obtain. So we have a universe without length and eternity is without end. Perhaps, we are recycled so that individually we may confront the history of man.

Parson scratches his head in bewilderment. Sunshine perks up intently.

Sandy And the Ankh and the helix, the old ends.

Akmed Conventionally so, but for us it is meaningless and we cannot know for we are sent where history has been, even where it will be for in the recycling process we are tense sensitive. We may precede our past or anticipate our future by the next assignment.

Sunshine	Well, Akmed at least you have a sense of the concepts of the Law of Conversation of Matter (or energy) and a religious corollary, the Pool of Souls idea. Matter is neither created nor destroyed only changed in form.
Dominique	Hold on now. Our bodies are put in the ground all of us under headstones.
Sandy	Or in the sea.
Sunshine	We corrupt into other usable forms. No different than a shed snakeskin—snake leaves skin behind, snake moves on.

Dominique shudders and trembles. Parson is wide eyed and still messing with his hair.

Dominique	I get chills. Reminds me of Drambulla-the snake god. Don't mention snakes. No more. I ain't got my same powers.
Sunchine	Well, Akmed is no Diego Rivera but the mural talks to us. Ought to have a name. What shall we call it, Akmed?
Akmed	Call it NONSENSE. Nothing makes sense now since we can't know the overall design of it. Call it Nonsense.
Sunshine	Looks like my damn tree needs fertilizer.
Sandy	Have a beer. From the sounds outside, I'll bet a bunch are leaving the blue room. Won't be long before they will

	be bound for us. Guess we aren't long from disposition ourselves.
Parson	Maybe some of dem are headed for the fields. Might be, I get to meet em. I'm lonely, been lonely. My Bess she plumb give out after thirty years of picking.
Sword	Hold on. Blue room. I was there once before here and in a red room and a green one too as I recall.
Sunshine	There's a pattern to it. Red, for lust, pain, adventure. That's where we started, green for impatience, envy or jealousy, pride, blue for melancholy and dissatisfaction. All of us have been in each room at different times.
Sandy	That is our commonality. We have all been on the same path—a path it seems without salvation.
Parson	No sir. He made us a promise. He said, we would be born again and he kept the promise.
Dominique	Yea, parson, but I don't remember him saying you will be born again, and again and again. Weren't too clear on that point.

Sandy chuckles and sword laughs. Parson asks Dominique why they are laughing.

| Dominique | They laugh you old fool because all of us misinterpreted the message. |

Now, sunshine laughs as well.

Sandy	My god, that's it. That's our commonality.
Sunshine	I am reminded of the old ancient Greek idea of the self-consuming snake who bites his own tail thus forming a circle—the Ouruborous. Curious looking symbol. For some reason alchemists used it. For the ancients it signified the eternal cycle of existence. It would seem our travels are circular and common
Sword	Common, yes and no. That's part of it. The severity of our deaths depended upon the intensity of our emotions in the other rooms. Some of us died a bit easier than others But violent nontheless. Yet, what of this room?
Sandy	I'll bet, love, happiness, promise. What we will have in the next life—the prize, the assignment that each of us is expecting. That's why it had the smiley faces on the walls that is before Akmed painted it.
Dominique	And we truly are deserving.
Parson	Amen.
Dominique	I know happiness is not allowed but we can have things. Sunshine has a tree. I want something.
Sandy	What then?
Dominique	I want a flower.

She snaps her fingers and a vase full of bright yellow Goldenrod appears on the stool next to her.

Sunshine	A damn weed. Ask for a flower get a damn weed. That's what we should expect. It figures!
Parson	Dat aint no weed. Dat ober my grave. Fer as the eye can see in dem southern fields. Dat and the Susan and de blackberry and de cotton. Goldenrod be my flower. Shore nuff.
Dominique	And mine. Sandy what would you want?
Sandy	Guess, I want to sail again but on calm seas like the one I remember being gently rocked upon.
Sunshine	He wants to crawl back in the womb. Cowardly!

Sandy ignores the insult.

Sandy	I get closer to the old "don't rock the boat" philosophy—a Chinese quietness philosophy. Let what happens be Hamlet's philosophy at his end.

An insect crawls into the room from under the door gap.

Parson	What's dat?
Sandy	Where?
Akmed	Over there on the floor. It's a centipede, see the legs. He is crawling toward the shade of Sunshine's tree.
Dominique	Do you think it knows where it is going?
Sandy	Ah, comon, do you think it cares?

The centipede continues to slowly crawl toward Sunshine's tree which seems to offer a paltry bit of shade.

Sandy By instinct, he seeks a sanctuary

Sword By reason, we seek the same. I think instinct must be better.

Sandy Why?

Sword	Instinct is reactionary. An animal senses danger and reacts. He doesn't plan for it. Our little fellow didn't think I'll seek safe shade. He saw it was there and he reacts to it.
Parson	Yessir, dat little fellow, he ain't got a care in dis here worl. The centipede has almost reached the edge of the shade where Sunshine sits. He lifts his leg and crushes the insect beneath his boot.
Dominique	Why the hell did you do that for. You low life Buddhist washout?
Sunshine	You watch your tongue. I'll be going on my next assignment soon and I don't want a damn insect hitching a free ride. Besides he's better off. Nothing in here for him. And I got dominion, I can do what I damn well want.
Parson	What dat word mean?
Sandy	In the bible, it says, I think in Genesis that man has dominion over the flora and fauna. In short, he can

do what he damn well wants with the insect. Legal by prescriptive permission but wrong on the face of it from my view.

Dominique   And mine.

Sandy   Sunshine, we are all screwed up. None of us are worth saving. Certainly, not me and most certainly not you. You killed the only damn diversion we had.

Sunshine   Big deal, I killed an insect. Saved, you say. From what? Haven't you been squashed already and how many times more to come. Waiting for a boot now, you are. He was lucky. One time. No test to see if you are worthy. No eventual relief from bondage with a great reception party when its over. Cause, its never over unless you are a poor damn dumb, instinct driven insect.

Sunshine sighs—worn out from the explanation. I did the little shit a favor. Now leave me alone.

Sunshine closes his eyes and soon begins to snore. Dominique flips him off and Parson begins to pray for him and the insect.

Parson   (sadly) Lawd, Mr. Sunshine, he don't mean what he say. And da little fellow dat he send yore way, takes care of em, please. Lord, where we's bound fer?

Hell, always hell, mumbles Dominique. Sandy pops his fingers for a drink as does Dominique.

At midnight, a peace comes over the room as each person begins to reflect on his own situation, on his own transient mortality.

Later, after a number of absences in the room. Akmed begins to figit. He is bored and wants to do something to pass the time. He yells to the others.

Akmed   Hey, wake up. Let's have a wager.

Sword   To what end?

Akmed   To see if centipede comes back

Sandy   Nonsense!

Akmed   Don't be so sure. Mythology has many examples of souls transformed into animals. Hell, that might have been ole headless from down the room a ways. Wasn't Agamemnon transformed into an Eagle. Even gods were transformed. I remember Zeus as a swan.

Sandy   You sure that is how it went?

Akmed   Something like that, what the hell does it matter. You got anything better to do?

Sword   Why should his death be final and ours not? Why should a centipede be luckier than we are when he is beneath us in the animal kingdom? I say take the wager.

Sandy   The wager?

Akmed   It can't be open ended because some of us might not be here if he eventually comes. So we must agree that the Centipede comes within a certain time period. I say an hour. He is shorter and he will be quicker to complete his mission.

Sunshine   If he has one.

Sandy   An hour then. What is the consideration?

Parson   What dat be?

Sandy   (looking to parson) Value of the bet?

Akmed   Hell, we'll play for funzies.

Dominique   Why not. Like you said, we ain't got nothing else to do

Sandy is engrossed in thought and mumbles time. Then he snaps his fingers and says hourglass. He hands the hourglass to Akmed.

Sandy   Well start her off.

Aknmed turns the hourglass upside down and sets it on the floor. A short time later. Parson is praying and still mumbling about the poor centipede. Sandy is still drinking sake and Dominique and Sword are quiet but intently looking at the hourglass. Suddenly, Dominique starts screaming.

Sunshine laughs at her and Akmed starts to advance on him.

Sandy   Dominique what is wrong? Why are you shouting?

Dominique   Can't you see. It is the end of the world. The sands in the hourglass have not moved. Not a grain has dropped through.

Sandy	It does not move because time is a real-time event. We are not.
Akmed	Right, dead, we are as inert and motionless as are the sands trapped within the hourglass. Contained there as surely as are we in the waiting room
Sunshine	Whether the centipede is recycled back to us within the hour or not is immaterial. The wager cannot be played.
Parson	Why?
Sunshine	Because time has no relevance to the dead.
Akmed	Nuts! One cannot repeatedly die without a sense of humor for the pathos of it—the unfairness. Shall we play a game?

No one speaks. No one smiles. Sandy is beginning to notice that Dominique attracts him. He is admiring her legs through the tear in her dress. Sunshine kicks his tree as if to stop the limbs from dropping. He mumbles that shock works on most things which triggers a response from Akmed.

Akmed	Are you shocked by this?

Akmed removes his head and rolls it on the floor so that it stops at Sunshine's hand.
Dominique screams. Horrified, Sunshine stares at the head. The eyes are open and the face bruised and blotched with blood.

Akmed	That's how it looked when the sword severed it. Well, I seem to have your attention, Mr. Sunshine.

Sunshine	Only a sick SOB would pull such a stunt. It is hideous. remove it.
Akmed	We can have a game. The Iroquois used to use severed heads for a game that was like lacrosse or soccer some type of ball game. When the head wore out, they would choose another. Usually, a fresh one.

He laughs uproariously. Dominique screams, get rid of it. Now! Sandy points to the head and snaps his fingers and the head disappears. Parson has the head in his hands. He mumbles, Lawd, where we's bound fer?

Akmed	What's wrong with a little dead head game in a room full of dead-heads?
Sword	Your coming on a little strong for us, my friend
Parson	Dat what we be—dead heads. Yes sir, we bees dat Shore nuff.

Akmed has a new head. He loosely combs his hair with the back of his hand. Sword swears at Akmed and studies Dominique. His attention to her is not lost on Sandy who frowns at him.

Parson Mr. Sandy, does you tink dat poor pede know he ded? When I was ded, I was here fore it figured on me. What be left on him but dat smudge. I remembers my grave.

Lest, I had a place, edge of a field. Hit were covered with goldenrod, pretty. He gots nuttin. By and by dat smudge be gone like him weren't here.

Dominique	(to Parson) Shut up you old fool. Damn insect is dead. Unlike us, final dead. Shut up!
Parson	Truth be. I long for my grave. Think on it sometimes.

Got pretty St. Augustine grass on the top of it. To rest, appeals to me. I'm tired of this undead feeling. I fancy hearing zombies call to me.

Sandy snaps his fingers for another Sake. He is a bit unsteady. Dominique sips her beer then spits it out.

Dominique	Beer got hot. Damn it tastes like piss. I need a rum and coke with ice. Dark rum, much ice.

In the background, they hear a tune. Parson starts to clap his hands. Dominique joins him. Sandy begins to hum a bit off key. Down further in the room the elderly men quit playing with the matchbox cars and are singing and clapping along.

Parson	I knows dat song. It be the speckled bird song. Ride to heaven on dem wings. Lawd, will send him fer me by and by, I spect.
Sandy	What the hell is Parson saying?
Dominique	The song is an old country music classic with lyrics about a lone speckled bird—a spiritual about him taking people to heaven. I love the lyrics. Story in Jeremiah. Seen birds like that in Louisiana and Texas. They call them the tulle goose. Also, speckled belly goose. Pretty!
Sword	Well, heaven or hell any bird will take you there.

Parson is still singing and clapping his hands and singing even though the tune has stopped.

Parson	Gwain to heaben, I is, ride dat bird straight to de Lawd.
Sunshine	I'm about to get my craw full of him. Can't you shut him up? Only ride we got cumin is that old Za-penng. Snap your butt back hard like a neck at the end of a noose.
Dominique	"Sword, I am curious what was your most difficult battle?"
Sword	"Chickamauga, in the Civil War." There in a dark thicket, tall trees so thick we could not see. We fought our hearts out We had some bad, indecisive generals and also one or two worth his salt but it wasn't the battle that depressed us so badly. We charged with the old rebel yell and scared hell out of the blue bellies.
Doninique	What then?
Sword	We were thirsty. The muddy Chickamauga creek where the battle stared soon was bloody—a blood-muck mess. Even flesh blown away by cannon shot or mini-ball was all about and in the water. Undrinkable, as Coleridge Said, "Water, water everywhere nor any drop to drink", something like that. Never have I been so thirsty.

Sword snaps his fingers and says, Chickamauga water. He holds in his hand a muddy glass of water tinged with blood and says drink anyone? How about a drink from the River of Death.

Parson	My Jesus, he would make dat water clear.
Dominique	Parson, maybe you ought to stop that preaching for a while.
Sunshine	I am interested Sword, how did a black get to fight on the side of the rebs. I know there were colored units like the 107th for the North but few I think for the South. How did you manage to fight at Chickamauga?
Sword	General Forrest put us to work. Confederate Congress had ordered that all backs captured should be sent back to their owners but mine had freed me and I had the papers. Those in limbo were supposed to be sent to Mobile to work on those fortifications but so much happened and so quickly that a few of us wound up with some of the reb units. Unlike the Northern colored units, we were pretty much disorganized So I fought with the Army of the Tennessee and I'm proud of it. I was colored then but still proud like the parson, I guess.
Sunshine	Why, proud?
Sword	My master had been decent. I liked the South and like Parson, I liked some things about the South. I survived that battle but died of Malaria.
Parson	Dats right, South weren't so bad sometimes.
Sunshine	That's right, parson. Complaining won't help. All life is pain and suffering. To shake this bitter cyclicality you

must go to a higher plane. Contemplate—take your consciousness to another level by mental propulsion.

Besides, I understand why religions fail. Religions mimic myth. What religion needs myth will invent. Expect nothing more from the room of love than from the room of hate—the smiley faces are an abstraction not a promise.

Sandy	Dominique, you mentioned that you had a child. Were you married long.?
Dominique	Specter was born from the rape, as I told you but yes I was married for an eternity it seemed. He wasn't much, a discontent a wanderer. Ours was a marriage of convenience and at the end a capitulation. I simply gave up. He came and went as he pleased, then he left. I survived by doing what women do in the face of necessity but I took no pleasure in it. What I would give to know the kind of love that gratifies—a caress as opposed to a shove. Oh god, how I do long for love.
Parson	Yea sister, we blacks got a special way with loving.
Dominique	Parson, have you ever seen the messenger?
Parson	Well yes, kinda have. Well, not I reckon seeing as you'd call it but once he came to the door and the room filled with a bright light as he pushed the envelope in for a fellow. I got on the floor and looked under the door gap and I seed his feet, he was sandaled and his feet had holes in them. Sister, light was in the holes in his feet. I seed it. Then I heard his voice. Oh it was soft, sweet like you'd begin a lullaby and he was crying.

Sword	Crying, you say?
Parson	Yessir, I think he don't much like his job. You know sending us back and all. I heard him say at least twice, Father, free them, father, free them. I know dats what he said.
Sword	Free us from what?
Sunshine	You idiots, from this continual merry go round, this bungee cord snapback. There is only one path to freedom and that is through nirvana. Let your mind be the catapult. Seek to be more than you can be and what you are will be meaningless, if achieved.
Sword	And if not achieved, we will continue to be exploited.
Sunshine	No, if not achieved you will continue to ooze through history and chronology will be useless as it too is a convenience. One day you may be yesterdays peasant, today's criminal or even tomorrows politician. Who knows but here is one constant if nirvana is not achieved, pain, misery and discontent will follow you to every way station.
Dominique	Yea, o.k. Sunshine, have you been anything but an oriental?
Sunshine	Yes, I was a Negro once during the time of the American Civil War. The Emancipation Proclamation said I was free but I didn't know what free meant.

Parson   Still don't!

Sunshine ignores Parson but gives him a disapproving glance and continues. Sandy pops his fingers for another sake.

Sunshine   Somehow, I strayed into a battle at Shiloh which means place of peace and I was run through by a bayonet—one of those triangular sided ones. Hard death. I coughed up my own blood and choked on it. No peace in the peach orchard just death and suffering. A free man for the first time died in a place of peace.

Sandy   Hell, freedom like time is a convenience, a convention as is that chronology you spoke about. Some Chinese philosophies advocate an acceptance, a quietness—a kind of don't rock the boat philosophy but I would fight to free these bonds. I swear I would. This Za-penng whip about grates on my nerves. I was buried but I don't stay buried. Enough to drive a man nuts. Might as well be a damn vampire.

Sword   Might get that chance later. Dominique could help us with the mechanics. Couldn't you gal?

Dominique takes off her hat and waves it at him but says nothing. Sandy continues.

Sandy   Parson must have been wrong in what he thought he heard the messenger say.

Parson   "Nawsir, Mr. Sandy, I knows what I heared. I sure does.

Dominique   Quiet, I hear him coming.

Sandy   Long ago sailors worried that they could sail off the edge of the Earth, now men worry that the universe is galloping away and there still is controversy over whether the earth will end in fire or ice as the poet said. Whatever earths end, whether by fire or ice that moment will meet us in one of the waiting rooms.

The room fills with a bright light. Akmed turns back toward the others. An envelope is pushed under the door with the name Tau 742p on it.

Sandy   I have it. It says, Tau 742p. Sword, looks like it is for you. Could be the prize. Open it, quickly. Tell us.

Sword holds the envelope in his hand for a moment as if afraid to open it. Then he rips it open.

Sandy   What does it say, man?

Sword   My god, the prize. At last, I will have a long life. a new theatre. It says that I am to join a column of British soldiers. They are near the African mountain of Isandhlwanda. I am to soldier again.

Akmed   What color is the ticket? What color?

Sword   At last, I will be a white man. The ticket is white.

All appear stunned. A loud Za-penng is heard and Sword is gone. The light is beginning to fade away.

Sandy   Well there you are. He got the prize. He is going to be a
               white man. Finally for him—a happy life!

Sunshine is laughing uncontrollably. He is slapping his hands on his legs.

Dominique   What the hell are you laughing about?

Sunshine   None of you know your history. He is going to fight in
               the Zulu war as a brit. A fracas enough to suit him but
               a bad end.

Akmed Why? The British won.

Sunshine   Not at Isandhlwana, the entire 24th column afoot
               was wiped out by Zulus under the command of the
               chieftain, Cetewayo. His red blood will stain that red
               jersey and that white pith helmet. Zulu spears will carve
               up his insides while he watches. His will not be an easy
               death—that is the legacy of the smiley faces—pain and
               suffering but there is the bright side, we get used to it."
               He will die and go back to the red room and start over,
               I suspect.

Parson   But you don't know that.

Sunshine   Cling to your hope, if you must. Red room, his next
               stop.

Dominique is crying again. Her vase of goldenrod is wilted and browned.
Sunshine's tree is devoid of leaves and dead.

Sunshine Ah, quit your crying little Voodoo lady. I should have remembered
myself and should have warned you not to want that goldenrod.

Dominique Why the hell not?

Sunshine   You don't see, I know. The plants are dead because the
                they are not the right kind of plant. Know this on your
                next visit to the room. The only plant that can grow in
                Hell is a pomegranate.

Parson lays down on his cotton bowls. Sandy pops another sake and
Sunshine begins to break the dead branch over him and shuts his eyes.
Dominique sobs and runs to Sandy. All now realize that the white ticket
is no more a ticket to peace, happiness or freedom than the red, blue or
green tickets were. They hear the messenger as he turns away from their
door and heads toward the red room. He speaks in a soft, pleading voice.

FATHER, FREE THEM

FATHER, FREE THEM, ALL

CURTAIN FALLS

SHORT FICTION
POEMS
AND
PARABLES

NOTHINGNESS AND TIME

I cannot easily conceive of nothingness,

A vacuumed bottle, no visible content, yet

There is something in the nothingness—air or spirit.

Was my mind ever empty? I remember nothing

From within the womb yet there were archetypes—

Instructions otherwise how would I as a toddler

Know to fear the snake before me. In the void before

The big bang, before time, what? Perhaps, God yawned

Before he began creation and that surge of breathe which

Preceded the explosion was in reality when time began.

The moment before the moment is forever lost as is

The Ineffable Word that the desert travelers sought.

GESTALT

(Assembling the dead at the last battle at Megiddo) I wandered among the dead seeking the orbit to which an orphaned eye belonged. Positions revealed a desperate struggle—bodies strewn about in haphazard manner. Some battle as yet unrecorded. This puzzle has many parts. I must accessorize by sequence, by elimination, by comparison—this leg to that legless one, yet, here a hand that must wait for there are several outstretched and each as worthy and one with his flip-off finger pointed upward toward heaven. Even the dead manifest their opinion with body language. The rude cut by sword, the spattering from a mortar, I must match the bone shard to the splinted bones in each. Much time required and already the crop is ripening. It is a fragmented site yet once all the parts are home we will have a whole. It will be greater than imagined, a remarkable achievement. Yet, the conclusion will be shifting, sifting in consciousness like loose sand upon which the footing is unsure. We will seek an answer but it will be shocking—only a truth inferred from the collection of the dead. We will embrace it as a constant, an unassailable revelation yet as it was based upon the inert it will be fallacious.

THE PROPHET

I cannot blow out the candles. There are too many and my breath is abbreviated. As I wait, I review the sequences of my life, starts and stops, panorama and vignettes, sweeping across the memory-swept plain of my tormented mind.

I was surrounded by momentous events that I ignored—all the flak that was Watergate, Woodstock, wars—insertions and extractions, insurgency and counter—insurgency even the riotous clamor of ethnic demands—the unsatisfied proponents of the word of God as recounted by men who only heard tales of the event. Thus was there continuous bickering and splintering over the intent of HIS word as if anyone knew the intent and assuming that the word as written did accurately reflect the intent.

Through it all I was content to be ordinary. Then I was startled by 9/11. I realized that even as a non-participant even comatose as I had been with respect to the noise, I was nonetheless a part of the happenings. Like cosmic radiation the ennui surrounded me. I needed a prophet with ties to the land and visions of the future, a prophet who had though the years gnawed at my subconscious—listen to me, hear me.

Like Rip I awoke to a world much changed. I had been at the center of the activity but oblivious to it. The Sunday school prophets that I learned of could not help me now. I needed a prophet of my youth to help me understand the meaning of my cationic state. Perhaps, in his words I would find a contemporary meaning to my election to withdraw, to opt out of this inflammatory process of a civilization in its death throes and I could then decide whether to sleep again.

I need to listen to Bob Dylan.

WHAT THE CONCH SHELL WHISPERED

You could decipher the whisper?

Oh yes, like Siegfried, I am able to hear the stories that animals tell-understand their language.

What did it whisper?

The Conch begged for help, for relief, compared the halcyon days of the pirate ships to the monstrous cruise ships that park in his lagoon. I remember the pleading word for word. It said:

> You cannot see my flesh. I am swollen with edema.
> Never before have I had such enemies as air and water.
> The Brain Coral shudders and convulses, the kelp suffers
> from the pesticide run-off and grows too fast, the clownfish
> no longer smiles, the crab no longer relishes the carrion that
> it feeds upon and I am horse. You, I blame.

Why did the conch blame you?

Because as a member of the company of men, I permitted this assault upon the conch and his friends. In the process of destroying ourselves, we have destroyed them.

You are not too blame for the world is still grand. Life remains the great adventure.

And death, the great tribulation. All you say is true but our greatness diminishes. I remember when Voltaire satirized the "Best of all possible worlds" in Candide. Well, we are great but by your account not as before. Besides man, his faults, his effects upon others, point out to me some evidence of something that was greater before than now. Something you recall as a triumph of nature in harmony with man—a pre-silent spring observation, please. What do you remember?

I remember when the conch shell still roared.

MAMMY

There is a song, terribly sad, that says something like "there ought to be clowns". Hell yes! I finished reading, The Catcher in the Rye when I got to thinking about that song. Holden, the young boy could not define himself or his place in the world and felt ambitiousness. He was, as I am, experiencing a grand ennui with life.

All the ancient philosophers, the many religious that I have studied never prepared me for the realization that all my efforts were of little consequence. Why? Because all our efforts revolve around absolute dichotomies such as night-day, birth-death, sleep-wake, hell-heaven, happiness-unhappiness and finally success-failure.

I was a nomad in thought even while I was rooted in deed, I wandered with my mind. All I wanted was to have some concrete revelation of purpose. What the hell was this toil, this strife worth and to what end? Not why man was here but why was I here.

I lived my life hitchhiking on a dream. I knew laughter and tears, plenty of both. Now, at the end of this horrid joke (as it seems sometimes), I feel the need to laugh. I've cried enough. All the things that I've seen, my God. My south has lost its identity, all her traditions decayed, her cotton fields turned into section eight housing for those who can't or as is often the case, won't work. My country has lost sight of the founding fathers principles and teeters on the edge of moral collapse. And just when it seemed that there might be hope for peace at the end of a great war more came. Three conflicts are active now and many more in ferment. We drift toward a certain Armageddon.

I can mark my life with many currents but the one that comes most to mind is the damn Civil Rights struggle. As most great moral campaigns go it stretched beyond the right. It reminds me of the speech from Orwell's Animal Farm which paraphrased said that "All animals were equal but some were more equal than others". And when emancipation became the mandate and the norm the escalation of it caused the pain.

History suggests that the more we progress the faster our acceleration toward the inevitable. It is generally accepted that great empires fall from within. And so, sing me a sad song but with meaning, a song that suggests the duality in which we are inextricably caught. We need a song that underscores our collective tragic history as a people. It's time for the clowns.

And as I lay in that final definitive clutch of death and gasp those last raspy painful breaths. Let me see a clown. Not any clown but one that reminds me of the South I loved, of a time when moral rectitude was not weighty on me as a personal issue, when I was prime and full of hope and purpose.

Bring me the clown I remember from my youth painted in blackface as was Al Jolson and signing as he did, MY MAMMY

THE JUBILEE

The Jubilee is one of those natural happenings that
Occurs on the banks of some southern bays where by
Some unique combination of tide, wind and low dissolved oxygen
Content in the water, a plethora of flounder, shrimp and crabs
Seemingly stunned lay close to the shore and can be gigged.

A young boy has wandered away from his parents and
Is about to gig a large flounder. He watches as a large star
Falls into the bay. At the same time, two people dressed in
Purple robes come by and stop. Both persons have
Crownes on their heads.

Well, young fellow have you gigged anything? Your name, please?

Yes, one flounder. I would have gigged a bigger one but you came.

My name is Wesley.

We are hungry, said the woman. Have you anything to eat?

I ate my last banana moon pie before you came up but you can have my Flounder to eat.

The boy reaches down and unties his stringer and offers to to the man.

Thank you, no. It is customary for us to reward good behavior. So little of it these days. Go to yonder hill where you will be safe.

Safe, in this tempest? Did you see the giant star that fell nearby?

Yes, its name is Wormwood. So go now, quickly. You will see us in the surf momentarily. Then you will understand. Another waits on the hill who offered kindness. Go now, you will make a lovely couple.

I need to find my parents.

Go now. When the sea is bruised and the rocks crumble from the teeth of the waves, look down from the hill and admire our catch. Our stringers should be full by then.

The water turned violent. The blue-black waves rose and devoured the shoreline. The boy climbed to the hilltop and sat down by the fire that a young girl had built.

Later the boy heard someone call to him so he walked to the ledge and looked down upon a hideous sight.

Stay where you are until the waters recede, Wesley. The woman yelled. What are your names?, he asked.

Jove and Juno, was the reply.

Have you caught many?, Wesley asked.

Oh yes, many. The wicked must perish. It is written. You and the girl will replenish and reestablish all that was in better form. You are our gift to a new world. See our catch so that you may remember the price of wickedness.

Wesley, looked down and watched in horror as Jove and Juno each raised a stringer from out of the angry surf. At the head of each was one of his parents and below them were long lines of gigged men.

JAZZ

I have never been able to dissect jazz
Or grasp a semblance of meaning from the
Rambling excursion up and down the scales.
It seems so vectorless yet there is a supposed
Rhythm-a disguised purpose. I can't discover the
Theme. The fault is mine. I seek simple fact
Apparent truths in all disciplines even music
A simple explanation of existence like Gershwin's
Rhapsody or Descartes resolution of I am.
Why should I wonder or care that the substance
Is veiled. I cannot label the paradoxes in life nor can
I anticipate the melody that death will reveal.

DESTINATION

A soul suddenly released from

    Mortal imprisonment

Is like a seed buffeted by the wind which

    Will settle when the breeze releases it

Yet, the seed which will often foster life

    Cannot choose its own destination

Neither can the soul which alights in some

    Unknown but predetermined manner

Yet, wherever seed or soul take root

    The rebirth will be cause

For grave concern.

2012

I will stare directly into the frightful void,

the indefinable spatial abyss now aligned

I will be reborn when my wobble is completed

when the spin marking my descent into madness

is done. The peril will challenge reason as did Y2K.

Man will no longer recognize culture or pretend to ethics

but content himself with the eschatological, existential, event.

Prayer, incantation, dance and rhetoric will not prevail.

I eschew all that frailty and enter the dark cave

where the fissure permits a gaseous exchange.

I emerge secure with the revelation into the searing sun

but distraught leave it, willingly leave it and renter the cave

and in the firelight recognize the familiar, friendly shadows

that flit, flirt and float against the foreboding wall.

THE LITTLE CHURCH AT CODEN

A gnarled old oak draped with unkempt Spanish moss

Still stands like a skeleton sentinel before the

Diminutive church of Coden

Reminiscent of legendary fishing communities like Gloucester

New Bedford, and Nantucket. Tiny Coden is

Nestled near a small estuary

Its proud folk reveal faces like the oak which reflect the

Weathering of hard times

The pastor said the Baptism and service was a sacred gift

Of a church to its parishioners—the best of all sacraments.

I saw smiles from aged, gray haired men with muscles still taunt

Shaped by a lifetime of toil with net and rigging. Despite its brevity

And simplicity the service was yet remarkable lacking the pomp,

Formality and circumstance of better financed worship sites.

It reminded me of the few intrepid Christians who first held their
 brief services in dank catacombs and darkened corridors.

In the recessed tiny hamlet of Coden

This service was most appropriate warm, relaxed, buoyant and

Vibrant with promise entirely as God meant a service to be.

MIDDLE EARTH

I am near the terminus of my wretched life

The reflection of my sins is but a minor discomfort

Nothing so permeates a man's existence as entropy

The knowledge of an end shrouded in a promise

So much have I forgotten. I thirst for knowledge

Gnostic or otherwise therein was my comfort in life. It is

Painful not to recall the cry of anguish in Heart of Darkness

Or the last poignant existential lines of Invictus or for me

The agonizing worst to forget the lost language of

Middle Earth.

DISORDER

The clock face on the plaster wall

Stares me into an existential submission.

It blinks, no doubt the jerky mechanical

Advancement of time into the next minute.

I am reflective but grateful that I survived

Even this brief meaningless progression.

It blinks again as I advance closer

To the uncertainty of eternity.

I can't pray salvation my way

And I do understand that existence

Is mechanical. Together the bleached bones

And rusted tin of the clock face and me

Will prove the age old phenomena of entropy.

TENSE

I have fleeting memories of WAS

Hope lost among them

Light, ephemeral, pregnant expectations

Of my youth dashed as I evolved.

IS bothers me. I tremble and for me

It becomes the worst of the three

For it is momentous as it flees

It becomes rabid impulse—nothing more.

Instantaneous leaves no time for plans

Hope is restrained yet again

Unnoticed IS, morphs to FUTURE

And I cannot reflect or anticipate for the

FUTURE on birth reverts to IS

And sadly I realize that IS in its immediacy

Is all life ever WAS

RAGGEDY ANN

I regret that I frowned and turned away from her

Not one am I to flake or flinch at disturbing sights

Now I think on it as my stream of sand nears its end

I lived a colorful, combative, inquisitive Gnostic life

I lucked out with a fair hand and I played it well

She sat with spindle legs, a misshapen jaw, a bloated face

Full with a Jack O-Lantern smile and looked like a limp

Flesh colored Raggedy Ann doll, inert and confined to

A metal stroller but oh, her captivating enigmatic smile

Perhaps in response to hope of a promise sealed by blood

My face wrinkled and weathered as it was and taunt, contorted

Observed such imagined joy in wonder. How could she know, find

With such limited mobility what I could not in a long labored search

Unlike me, she had never been battle tested and I could not reflect

Her smile. I was a worn out warrior. She had been born a victim.

SHADOWMAN

Specter of an animated stickman

Shirking in the convoluted shadows

Fleshless, frightening, apparition

Pathetic, smirking, pale zombie

Heartless, soulless, creaking stick house

The breeze rattles thy flimsy frame

Rickety structure sway and fall

Be no more fright to me

You move me to remembrances

Deep in the corridors of my mind

I shudder to recollect a familiar resemblance

In the structure, in the void of thee

You remain the residue of me.

SORTING THROUGH PHOTOGRAPHS

I triage my fondest memories

Sort, augment, tincture, trim

Knead them like play dough

To suit a coming need

Like a rusted latch

Time defeats the utility

Of each thus the repair

My precious, personal remembrances

Collated, filed and bundled

In each, a younger frozen me stares

Back at its wrinkled, browned counterpart

Most of the worst, most painful images

Are thankfully dim, blurred and indistinct

I will leave them behind

And carry only the best as I leave soon

On my inescapable journey through eternity.

HEADSTONE

I only come here in the dread of winter

when the frost crackles beneath my feet

when I am numb from the ennui of life

I first look up to the distant hilltop

Where rest the chiseled praying hands

That regularly must be bleached and whitewashed

I come because the perpendicular headstones

Pot marked, weathered, and mildewed

Remind me of that special day with you

Before the wrinkles, loose skin and liver spots

Both of us in the flush fullness of youth

You sat astride me in a perpendicular aspect

Your weight breaking my brown grass

As we lay spent, you gently lifted away

Leaving scented droplets of warm dew

I could not come here in spring

Only in winter when the North wind

Howls, penetrates and scrubs the stones

The trampled brown turf lies inert beneath me

It is this harsh brittle envelope that surrounds

My perfect memory of that sprightly spring

When this desolate hillside was a wildflower meadow

Not yet contaminated with perfectly aligned stones

And last Judgment Day bodies in waiting

When we formed a headstone near the praying hands.

LEGEND OF THE CORN

He followed the ant into the

mountain and brought out the kernel of life.

CORN

Gift of the God

Quetzalcoatl, who retrieved it for us. In its golden coffin, lied a dormant corpse.

Bury him, until rot breaks into the capsule and permits the resurrection.

Corn mother birthed many and filled her allotted portion of the

Cornucopia.

It is known that corn waits until its hair is long, until its torso is strong and supportive, until the approval of the sun god is realized and then it offers its flesh to the indifferent users.

The humans decided it would be better utilized as food for the voracious, metal-monster, burden bearers who consumed with abandon and littered and polluted the graveyard of the corn which resulted in a massive apocalypse such that the great god retrieved the corn mother and returned her to the safety of the mountain. With Corn Mother thus hidden, the garden remained forever fallow. This is recorded in the last known Codex written in the 5th sun.

WE GO OUT OF A DARK TUNNEL

INTO A LIGHTED TUNNEL

AND IN-BETWEEN WE WANDER

THROUGH HEAVEN AND HELL

BOOKS BY PERRY L. ANGLE

Existential Musing of a Southern Individualist
Existential Ramblings of a Southern Individualist

The Butterfly Transport
(Poetic meditations on our collective conscious)

The Waiting Room Chronicles

Books by Perry L. Angle are available at Barnes and Noble.com,
iuniverse.com, Amazon.com and other internet book sites.
Existential Musing of a Southern Individualist includes Defiance,
the story of hunting camp individuals caught up in the drama of a
hurricane.
Existential Ramblings of a Southern Individualist includes a time-zone
letter to General Robert E. Lee and several southern short stories.

If you have enjoyed The Waiting Room, please tell others about the body
of work by this author.